PARROTS

Don't Live in the City!

Written by Lucy Reynolds

Illustrated by Jenna Herman

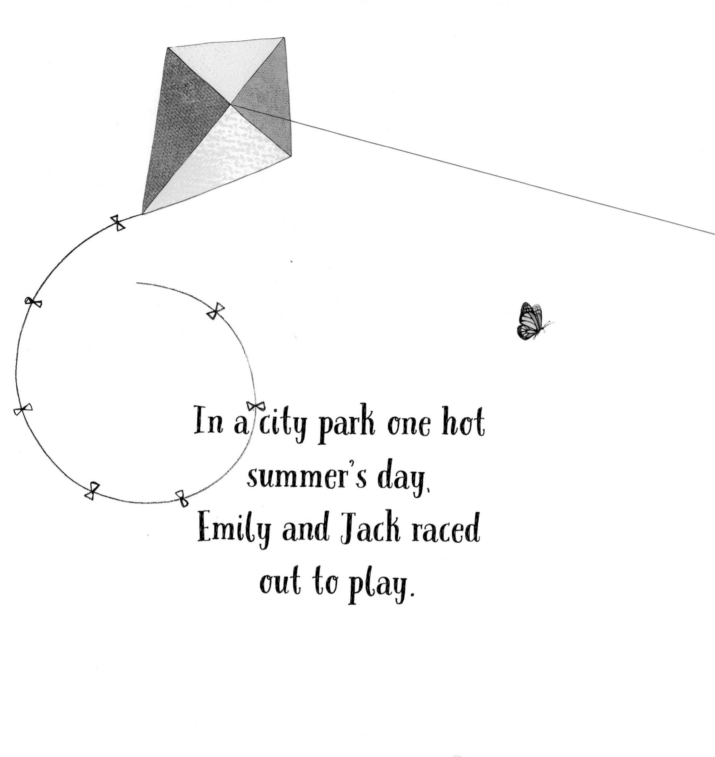

In a city park one hot
summer's day,
Emily and Jack raced
out to play.

They were flying their kite

loop-the-loop up high...

when something emerald flickered by.

'Look, it's a **parrot!**'
cried Jack in surprise,
as a green flash of feathers
flew through the skies.

But Emily laughed and
shook her head.

'Parrots don't
live in
the city!'
she said.

'There, in the bush!'
he called with a shout,

cheep cheep cheep

as a small amber eye like a
jewel peeped out.

Buzz hummed the bees,
the ducks went *quack!*
And Emily said,

'There's no parrot, Jack!'

'It's there in the tree -
its feathers are green,

it's the loveliest parrot
I've ever seen!'

But Emily looked at the flowers,

all colourful and pretty...

'There *really* are
n0 parrots
in the city!'

ribbit ribbit, ribbit ribbit

'There are!' Jack insisted. 'I saw one – it's true! I wonder if it escaped from a zoo?'

Emily sighed.

'You've been misled...'

'Parrots only live in the jungle!' she said.

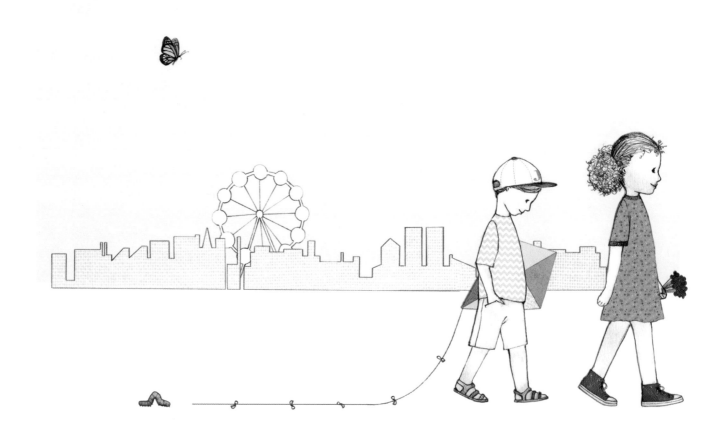

So slowly, sadly Jack trailed along,
thinking that really he must've been wrong.

'I'm sure I saw feathers;
I thought I saw wings,

but I guess I was only
imagining things.'

So he launched his kite back into the sky…

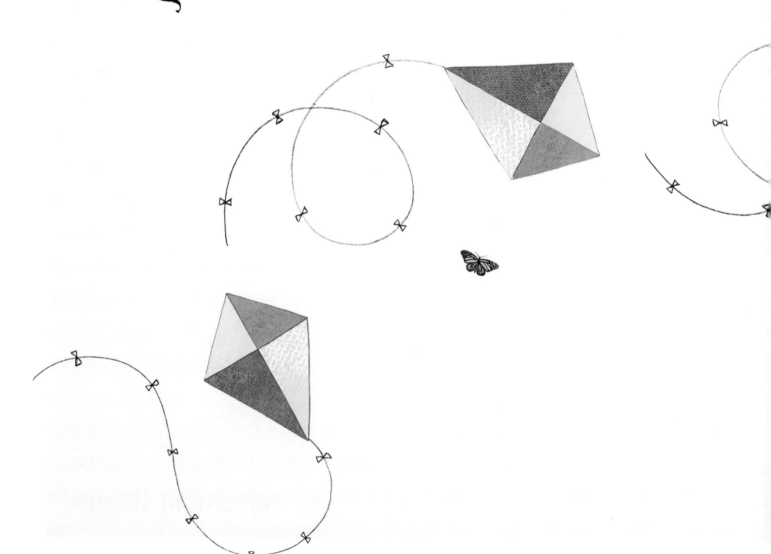

'til it crashed high up
in a tree nearby!

As it did, a great racket almighty and loud...

BURST
OUT
from the

branches

like a thunderous

cloud !

And the sky filled with parrots

pouring out from the tree, like

a bird-coloured rainbow

soaring free!

They flapped and they squawked
and they dived and they screamed,
streaking the sky with
shimmering green.

Then, fluttering and circling, screeching *kee-ak* and *kee-ee,*

kee-ee

kee-ak

they disappeared back inside the tree!

And Emily stood,
amazed and wide-eyed...

'You really *did*
see a **parrot**!'
she cried.

So next time you're out
and about for a walk,
look up in the trees and
listen out for a squawk.

Because even if
nobody else believes,
you *may* glimpse a shimmer
of green through the leaves!

THE END

PARROTY

Did you know, the birds that
Jack and Emily spot are called
'ring-necked' or 'rose-ringed' parakeets?
This is because of the collar of pink
and black they have around their necks.

Ring-necked parakeets are part of
the parrot family. They originally
come from the Indian subcontinent
and central Africa, but now thousands
of them live in cities all around
the world, in countries where they
wouldn't normally be found!

INDIAN
SUBCONTINENT

FILM:
Parrots Don't
Live in the City!

Nobody knows exactly how
the parakeets got to those cities!
Maybe they escaped from a zoo?
Or a pet shop? Or a film set?
How do you think they got there?

FUN!

They make very popular pets because they're good at mimicking human speech. They can learn to copy words and even imitate city noises like police car sirens!

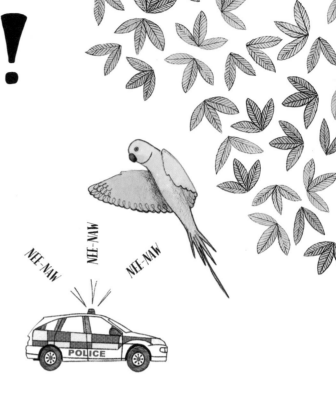

NEE-NAW NEE-NAW NEE-NAW

They like to eat buds, nuts, fruits, berries and seeds - perfect where there are lots of bird feeders in people's gardens! Can you spot anything in the book that the parakeets could have for their supper?

A group of parrots is called a pandemonium. They are very noisy flocks! Their call is a loud *kee-ak* or *kee-ee*, which they make while they're flying. Can you imitate this noise?

kee-ak kee-ak kee-ak

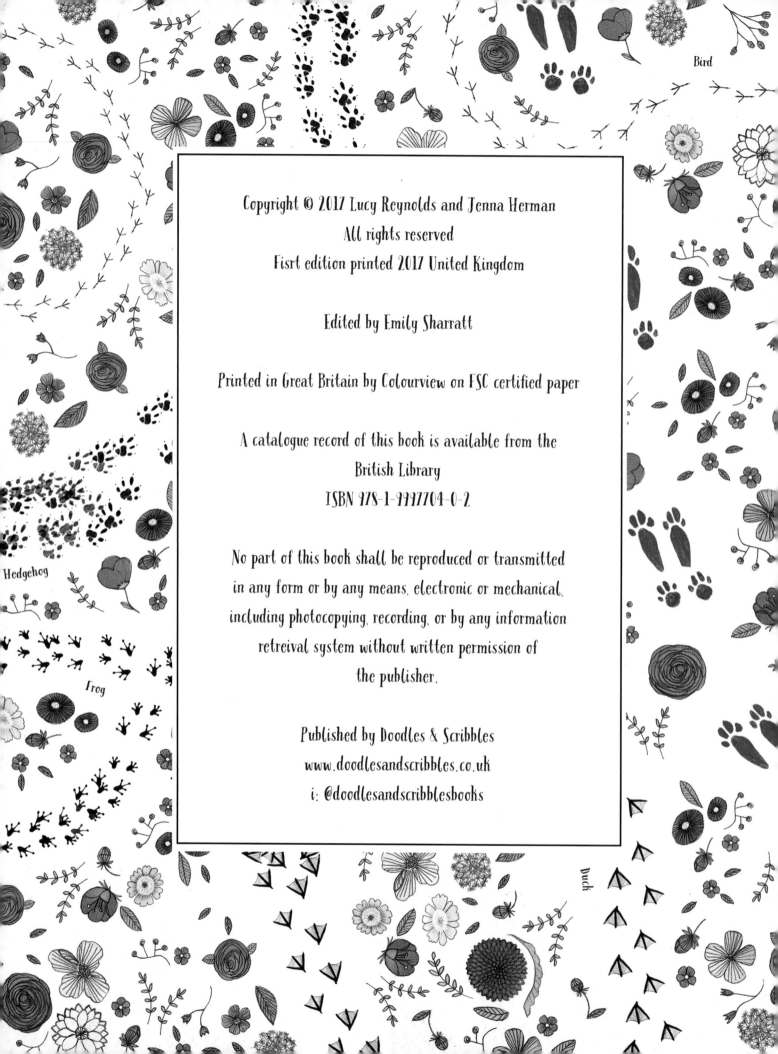

Published by Doodles & Scribbles
www.doodlesandscribbles.co.uk
i: @doodlesandscribblesbooks

Bird

Hedgehog

Frog

Duck